Lincoln Peirce

BIG NATE

MR POPULARITY

HarperCollins *Children's Books*

Also by
Lincoln Peirce

Big Nate: The Boy with the Biggest Head in the World
Big Nate Strikes Again
Big Nate on a Roll
Big Nate Goes for Broke
Big Nate: Boredom Buster
Big Nate: Fun Blaster
Big Nate: What Could Possibly Go Wrong?
Big Nate: Here Goes Nothing!
Big Nate Flips Out
Big Nate Doodlepalooza
Big Nate in the Zone

First published in Great Britain by HarperCollins *Children's Books* in 2014
HarperCollins *Children's Books* is a division of HarperCollins*Publishers* Ltd,
1 London Bridge Street, London SE1 9GF.

These comic strips first appeared in newspapers from August 10, 2009 through March 7, 2010.

www.harpercollins.co.uk

2

Text and Illustrations © 2014 United Feature Syndicate, Inc.

The author asserts the moral right to be identified as the author of this work.

ISBN 978-0-00-755927-5

Printed and bound in China

SIR STORYTIME

WHEN OPPORTUNITY KNOCKS...

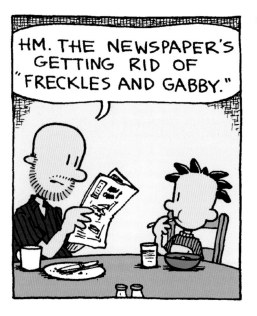

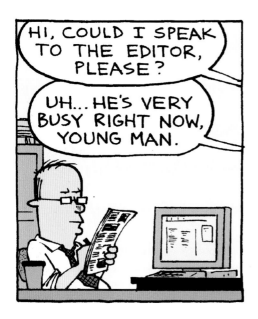

HERE'RE TWO WEEKS OF "DOCTOR CESSPOOL" STRIPS! THESE'LL GIVE YOU AN IDEA OF MY COMEDY STYLINGS!

DOCTOR CESSPOOL IS AN EMERGENCY ROOM SURGEON! WHAT A GREAT SETTING FOR A COMIC STRIP!

IT'S CHOCK-FULL OF ACTION, HIJINKS, AND HILARIOUS GAGS!

...THE KEY WORD BEING "GAGS."

RIGHT! AND JUST WAIT 'TILL I ADD **COLOUR!**

YOUNG MAN, I CAN'T POSSIBLY PRINT "DOCTOR CESSPOOL" IN MY NEWSPAPER.

WHAT? WHY **NOT**?

IT'S CRUDE, IT'S VULGAR, IT'S VIOLENT...

RIGHT! THAT'S WHAT SETS IT **APART**!

NO **OTHER** COMIC STRIPS FOLLOW THE WACKY ADVENTURES OF AN EMERGENCY ROOM SURGEON!

8/22

EXACTLY.

Ex**ACT**... WAIT, WHAT?

© 2009 by NEA, Inc.

Peirce

SHOP TILL YOU DROP

© 2009 by NEA, Inc.

LEARNING ≠ FUN

Here's a tip
for the youthful 6th grader...

...who considers himself
a school hater:

Though I'm mortar and brick,
and I can't run a lick...

I'll catch up to you
sooner or later.

PUBLIC SCHOOL 38
Est. 1918
WELCOME BACK
STUDENTS

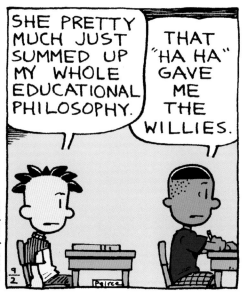

© 2009 by NEA, Inc.

GOOD SUB, BAD SUB

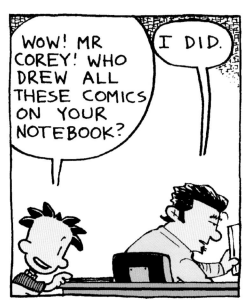

MR COREY IS THE BEST SUB WE'VE EVER HAD! HE'S COOL!

HE'S A **CARTOONIST**! I WAS JUST LOOKING AT SOME OF HIS DRAWINGS! THEY'RE, LIKE, TOTALLY **PRO**!

FINALLY WE'VE GOT A TEACHER WHO ACTUALLY KNOWS WHAT HE'S **DOING**!

HE JUST DEFINED AN ISOSCELES TRIANGLE AS A ZONE IN THE OCEAN WHERE SHIPS AND PLANES DISAPPEAR.

EX**ACT**LY! THAT'S KNOW-LEDGE WE CAN **USE**!

ZEROING IN

MR POPULARITY

ALL RIGHT, I'M GOING FOR IT! I'M RUNNING FOR CLASS PRESIDENT!

YES!

for IDENT

VOTE for ALISON

WHY SHOULD THE **POPULAR** KIDS BE THE ONLY ONES TO GET ELECTED?

EX**ACT**LY!

9/23

THEY MAY BE COOL AND SMART AND ATHLETIC AND TALENTED, BUT **YOU'RE**... UH.. YOU'RE... YOU...

© 2009 by NEA, Inc.

THINK HARD.

I GOT NOTHIN'.

Peirce

© 2009 by NEA, Inc.

9/30

...AND NOW HE SAYS HE DOESN'T **REMEMBER** STEALING THE MONEY! TALK ABOUT SELECTIVE MEMORY!

WHAT'S SELECTIVE MEMORY?

I'LL SHOW YOU!

NATE, WHO WON THE 2006 MTV VIDEO MUSIC AWARD FOR BEST HIP-HOP VIDEO?

BLACK EYED PEAS, "MY HUMPS".

IN "PEANUTS," WHAT WAS THE NAME OF CHARLIE BROWN'S BASEBALL HERO?

JOE SHLABOTNIK.

WHO WON "SURVIVOR: PALAU"?

TOM WESTMAN.

WHO WAS THE 1981 NBA FINALS MVP?

CEDRIC MAXWELL.

WHAT'S OUR MATHS HOMEWORK FOR TOMORROW?

HOMEWORK?

WAIT, WHAT?

SEE?

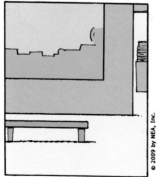

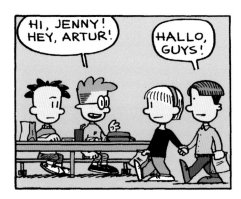

EL PRESIDENTE

AH! PRINCIPAL NICHOLS! JUST THE MAN I'M LOOKING FOR!

NOW THAT I'M SIXTH-GRADE PRESIDENT, I'LL BE NEEDING A PLACE TO DO BUSINESS! YOU KNOW, SORT OF A HEADQUARTERS!

SO!.... WHAT'S AVAILABLE IN TERMS OF OFFICE SPACE?

YOU WANT AN **OFFICE** FOR BEING ON THE **STUDENT COUNCIL?**

NOTHING TOO BIG. I COULD TAKE OVER THE STAFF ROOM!

© 2009 by NEA, Inc.

...AND I ALREADY SPOKE TO THE DIRECTOR OF THE SOUP KITCHEN, AND HE'S TOTALLY ON BOARD!

WONDER-FUL!

I'M **IMPRESSED**, NATE! YOU'RE SHOWING A LOT OF INITIATIVE AND LEADERSHIP! IT'S VERY... VERY...

10/22

...PRESIDENTIAL?

YES!

PERHAPS BEING A CLASS OFFICER WILL CHANGE HOW YOU...

OOP. GOTTA GO. I'VE GOT DETENTION.

NATE, I'M VERY PROUD OF ALL THE COMMUNITY SERVICE WORK YOU'RE DOING!

THANKS, DAD!

I THINK A LITTLE FAMILY CELEBRATION IS IN ORDER! HOW ABOUT I TAKE YOU OUT TO SUPPER?

SURE!

ANYWHERE YOU WANT TO GO! NAME THE PLACE!

10
23

© 2009 by NEA, Inc.

SUNSHINE

SOUP KITCHEN

VOLUNTEERS NEEDED

TRICKED OUT

MR FANCY-PANTS

SCHOOL PICTURE GUY!

YOWZA! NICE THREADS, KID! VERY SHARP!

YEAH, I DECIDED TO DRESS UP, SINCE I'M CLASS PRESIDENT THIS YEAR!

AH, ELECTED OFFICE! CONGRATS, AMIGO!

BUT I'LL WARN YOU, KID: POLITICS CAN BE A **VIPER PIT**! AS YOURS TRULY FOUND OUT NOT SO MANY YEARS AGO!

11/3

© 2009 by NEA, Inc.

YOU KNOW WHAT, I THINK I HEAR THE BELL...

JEALOUSY ABOUNDED WHEN I WAS NAMED CAPTAIN OF THE ROBOTICS TEAM...

Peirce

NATE, I'D LIKE YOU TO WORK ON YOUR LEFT HAND!

HM?

A GOOD POINT GUARD NEEDS TO DRIBBLE, SHOOT AND PASS WITH **EITHER** HAND!

COACH

ARRGH! I CAN'T DO **ANY**THING LEFTY! I KEEP WANTING TO USE MY **RIGHT** HAND!

I'VE GOT AN IDEA!

DRIBBA DRIB DRUB DRUB...

DUCT TAPE?

YUP! WE'LL TAPE YOUR RIGHT ARM!

THIS WAY YOU'LL **HAVE** TO USE YOUR LEFT HAND!

SHHK!

$\frac{11}{8}$

OK, OK. ISN'T THAT ENOUGH?

NOT YET. WE'VE GOTTA MAKE IT HOLD!

TWO MINUTES LATER...

I... WILL... KILL... YOU.

CATCH!

© 2009 by NEA, Inc.

Peirce

I'M ONLY TWO LOCKERS AWAY FROM **MARCUS** NOW! HE AND I ARE BECOMING **VERY** TIGHT!

AH! **MARCUS!** MY **MAN!**

IS IT JUST ME, OR DID IT SUDDENLY GET ALL DORKY AROUND HERE?

☆SNICKER!☆

HEAR THAT, FRANCIS? BEAT IT.

© 2009 by NEA, Inc.

SWISH

© 2009 by NEA, Inc.

105

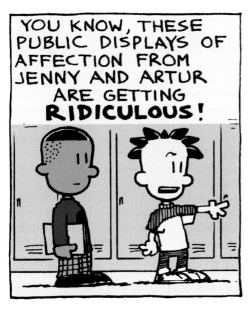

BON VOYAGE!

NATE. HALLO. HAVE YOU SEE JENNY?

JENNY? YOU MEAN SHE'S NOT WITH **YOU**?

GEE, ARTUR, THE TWO OF YOU ARE **USUALLY SUPER-GLUED** TO EACH OTHER, PLAYING **TONSIL HOCKEY!**

NO. IS IMPOSSIBLE, NATE, BECAUSE MY TONSILS WERE TO TAKE **OUT** WHEN I WAS YOUNGER!

THANKS FOR CLEARING THAT UP, ARTUR.

WHAT WE ARE **ACTUAL** DOING IS **KISSING!**

© 2009 by NEA, Inc.

MY FATHER IS PROFESSOR AT UNIVERSITY. HE IS GO TO BIG RESEARCH VACATION.

A SABBAT- ICAL!

YES. SO FOR NEXT SIX MONTHS I WILL TO LIVING IN ISTANBUL.

WOW! NO **WONDER** JENNY WAS UPSET!...

RIGHT! SHE KNOWS THAT SPENDING SO MUCH TIME APART WILL PROBABLY **DESTROY** YOUR RELATIONSHIP!

© 2009 by NEA, Inc.

IT WILL?

BON VOYAGE, ARTUR! TRY NOT TO GET AIRSICK!

12/5

© 2009 by NEA, Inc.

HI, NATE.

DAD, DO YOU THINK I'M TOO COMPETITIVE?

WHY DO YOU ASK?

FRANCIS SAYS I AM.

WELL, MAYBE HE HAS A POINT.

BUT WHAT'S WRONG WITH A LITTLE COMPETITION? THAT'S WHAT MAKES THE WORLD **WORK!**

COMPETING IS HOW YOU **SUCCEED!** YOU GET NOTICED BY BEING THE **BEST!**

I WANT TO BE THE BEST AT **EVERYTHING** I DO! THE BEST SOCCER PLAYER! THE BEST DRUMMER!

12/13

THE BEST STUDENT?

© 2009 by NEA, Inc.

HE WON THAT ONE.

DATE WITH DETENTION

FAIR-WEATHER FRIENDS

IT'S PRACTICALLY CHRISTMAS AND WE HAVEN'T HAD A SINGLE SNOWFLAKE! THIS IS TOTALLY UNACCEPTABLE!

I'M GOING TO CALL THE TV WEATHER GUY AND GIVE HIM A PIECE OF MY MIND!

BOOP BEEP BOOP BEEP

BUT IS MISDIRECTED ANGER IN KEEPING WITH THE HOLIDAY SPIRIT?

WHAT'S **THAT** SUPPOSED TO MEAN?

NEVER MIND.

THEY'RE PLAYING "LET IT SNOW" WHILE I'M ON HOLD! OH, THAT'S **HILARIOUS!**

© 2009 by NEA, Inc.

12/17

Peirce

HOW 'BOUT A NAPKIN ?

REALITY BITES

'TWAS THE NATE
BEFORE CHRISTMAS

SNOW BUSINESS

THANKS FOR NOTHING

I CAN'T FIGURE OUT THIS MATHS PROBLEM.

IT'S EASY, CHAD. I THINK YOU JUST ADD THOSE TWO GUYS THERE.

THEN YOU TAKE THAT NUMBER AND DIVIDE IT... NO, WAIT... MAYBE YOU **MULTIPLY** IT... BY THAT NUMBER. NO, THAT'S THE PAGE NUMBER. WHATEVER. NEVER MIND.

ANYWAY, AFTER THAT YOU HAVE TO FIND THE LOWEST COMMON DENOMI-THINGY...

THAT'S OK, DON'T WORRY ABOUT IT. I'LL FIGURE IT OUT.

SOME PEOPLE JUST DON'T WANT TO BE HELPED.

STILL STRUGGLING WITH YOUR HOME-WORK, CHAD?

CLASS STARTS IN FIVE MINUTES, AND I CAN'T GET THIS QUESTION!

MM-HMM... MM-HMM...

THE ANSWER IS SWINE FLU.

BUT IT'S A MATHS PROBLEM.

I MEAN FAKE AN ILLNESS. OTHERWISE YOU'RE TOAST.

© 2010 UFS, Inc.

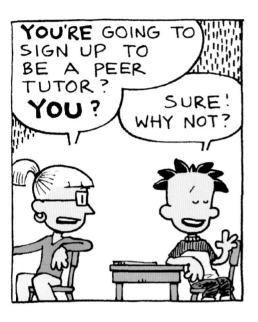

I CAN'T BELIEVE THEY MAKE YOU HAVE A B-PLUS AVERAGE TO BE A PEER TUTOR!

WHAT A BOGUS REQUIREMENT! WHY IS EVERYTHING ALWAYS ABOUT **GRADES**?

I BELIEVE IT WAS ARISTOTLE WHO SAID: "PEOPLE WHO WORRY ABOUT THEIR GRADES ARE **NIMRODS**"!

YES, THAT SOUNDS LIKE SOMETHING ARISTOTLE WOULD HAVE SAID. ...OR MAYBE IT WAS KANYE. WHATEVER.

I WAS THINKING ABOUT JOINING THE PEER TUTORING PROGRAMME...

...BUT THEN I FOUND OUT YOU NEED TO HAVE A B-PLUS AVERAGE TO BE A TUTOR, SO I CAN'T DO IT.

....UNLESS YOU WORK SO HARD THAT YOU **DO** HAVE A B-PLUS AVERAGE!

NAH.

© 2010 UFS, Inc.

Peirce

154

NATE WRIGHT, VIBE CONSULTANT

VIBES ARE EVERY-WHERE, FRANCIS. EVERYBODY'S GOT A VIBE.

WELL, **I** DON'T SEE ANY.

YOU CAN'T SEE 'EM WITH YOUR **EYES**, FOOL! VIBE IS SHORT FOR **VIBRATION!** YOU **FEEL** 'EM! YOU **SENSE** 'EM!

THAT'S WHAT **I** DO, ANYWAY! I HAVE THE ABILITY TO PICK UP ON PEOPLE'S VIBES **INSTANTLY!**

© 2010 by UFS, Inc.

1/12

THAT'S THE MOST RIDICU-

OOP. SKEPTICAL VIBE. LOUD AND CLEAR.

I'VE DECIDED TO CAPITALISE ON MY AMAZING ABILITY TO READ VIBES!

"NATE WRIGHT, VIBE CONSULTANT"?

YUP! THERE ARE TONS OF PEOPLE OUT THERE WHO HAVE NO **IDEA** HOW TO PICK UP VIBES!

FOR ONLY FIVE BUCKS AN HOUR, I CAN TEACH THOSE PEOPLE MY VERY SPECIAL GIFT!

© 2010 by UFS, Inc.

I JUST PICKED UP A MAJOR SLEAZE VIBE.

I DON'T PICK UP VIBES. I JUST LEAVE 'EM LYING THERE.

OK, CHAD, WE'VE GOT A LIBRARY FULL OF PEOPLE HERE! TRY TO PICK UP SOME VIBES!

OK.

WELL... I'M SENSING SOMEONE WHO'S NOT TOO SURE OF HIM-SELF... IT'S SORT OF AN AWKWARD, CLUMSY VIBE.

...AND SHY! I'M GET-TING A VIBE OF SOME-BODY WHO GETS NERVOUS IN CROWDS, WHO'D RATHER SPEND TIME WITH HIS MODEL TRAINS AND HIS LEGOS...

© 2010 by UFS, Inc.

YOU'RE PICKING UP YOUR OWN VIBE, CHAD.

...AND HIS ACTION FIGURES AND... WHAT?

THOMAS JEFFERSON, FOUNDING FATHER
By Nate Wright

Thomas Jefferson, a great American, was born on the historic day of April 13, 1743 in the sleepy little village of Shadwell, Virginia. Tom's dad was named Peter and his mum was Jane. When Tom was fourteen years old, his dad (Peter) died, so from then on Tom was in charge because his father was dead. Tom decided he wanted to go to college, but apparently there weren't many colleges around back then because the only one he could find had the very strange name of William and Mary. But he went there anyway. Also, during this time he learned how to play the violin. After college Tom got married. His wife was named Martha, which by coincidence was also the name of George Washington's wife Martha.

Anyway, married life must have been kind of boring, because Tom decided to get into politics. He was in the Virginia House of Burgesses and also was a member of the second Continental Congress. Tom drafted (which is a fancy word for "wrote") the Declaration of Independence, which was when the colonial guys told the British to give them their freedom. Writing the Declaration of Independence was the reason Tom was one of the founding fathers, which is why I called this essay "Thomas Jefferson, Founding Father." During the whole American Revolution thing, Tom was elected governor of Virginia. Then his wife died. What she died from, I have no idea. But obviously Tom got on with his life, because pretty soon after that he became a congressman. Then he became minister to France, so he spent a lot of time hanging around in Paris. And then George Washington, who was president at the time, hired Tom to be the secretary of state.

Tom ran for president in 1796, but he lost the election to John Adams, so he became vice president instead. Then in 1800 Tom ran again, and this time he won. So then he was president. He was the third president in United States history. Some of his major accomplishments that he did while he was president were the Louisiana Purchase and the Embargo Act. He also invented the University of Virginia.

After that, Tom just hung out and got old, and he died on July 4th, 1826, which is an amazing coincidence because that was the 50th anniversary of the Declaration of Independence, which Tom wrote as we all remember so well. So, to sum up the life and career of Thomas Jefferson, founding father (which is also the title of this essay): he was a congressman, a governor, a secretary of state, a vice president, and a president. Wow, that is truly incredible. Oh, and also Tom's picture is on a nickel. Thomas Jefferson will never be forgotten. It is so, so, so, so, so, so, so, so, so, so, so, so, so important that today's American citizens understand how very, very, very, very, very, very important he was.
THE END

THE WOMAN ASKED FOR A 500-WORD ESSAY, AND I **GAVE** HER A 500-WORD ESSAY!

SIT DOWN, SON.

© 2010 by NEA, Inc.

PRINCIPAL

17 Peirce

MOUSE!

HOW COME WE HAVE **MICE** ALL OF A SUDDEN? WHERE DID THEY COME FROM?

FROM OUTSIDE, I'D GUESS.

WHEN THE WEATHER GETS COLD, THEY LOOK FOR WARM SPACES WHERE THEY CAN LIVE AND EAT!

WHEREVER YOU FIND A LOT OF CLUTTER OR FOOD ON THE FLOOR, YOU'RE LIKELY TO FIND MICE.

1/20

© 2010 by UFS, Inc.

I'M GOING TO GO CLEAN MY ROOM.

BONUS!

Peirce

IF WE CATCH THE MOUSE, WHAT ARE WE GOING TO DO WITH IT?

WE'RE **NOT** FLUSHING IT!

IT MIGHT SWIM BACK UPSTREAM AND BITE ME ON THE BUTT WHILE I'M SITTING ON THE TOILET!

I NEVER THOUGHT OF THAT!

THAT'S YOUR PROBLEM, ELLEN. YOU DON'T THINK THINGS THROUGH RATIONALLY LIKE **I** DO.

"RATIONALLY." GOOD ONE.

LET'S JUST MOVE TO A DIFFERENT HOUSE.

Peirce

ARTUR ISSUES

I'VE BEEN HAVING WEIRD DREAMS LATELY.

OH, YEAH?

YEAH! **ARTUR** KEEPS SHOWING UP AND THREATENING TO PUNCH ME OUT IF I PUT THE MOVES ON JENNY WHILE HE'S IN TURKEY!

AH-**HA!**

YOU KNOW WHAT THAT MEANS?

OF **COURSE** I DO, FRANCIS!

IT MEANS THAT EVEN WHEN HE'S NOT AROUND, ARTUR IS INCREDIBLY ANNOYING.

RIGHT.

1-27

Peirce

TELL ME MORE ABOUT ARTUR, NATE.

HE'S NOT EVEN **AROUND** RIGHT NOW! HE'S IN TURKEY FOR SIX MONTHS.

DO YOU THINK THAT'S WHY YOU'RE DREAMING ABOUT HIM?

WHOA, **WHOA!** I'M NOT DREAMING **ABOUT** HIM!

I'M DREAMING ABOUT **REGULAR** STUFF, BUT **ARTUR**, IN HIS COMPLETELY OBNOXIOUS WAY, KEEPS SHOWING UP AND **SPOILING** EVERYTHING!

$\frac{2}{4}$

© 2010 by UFS, Inc.

THAT **DOES** SOUND OBNOXIOUS.

"DREAMING ABOUT HIM" MAKES IT SOUND LIKE I'VE GOT SOME KIND OF **ISSUE** WITH THE GUY!

OK, NATE, LET'S SEE IF I'VE GOT THIS STRAIGHT...

YOU'RE FRIENDLY WITH ARTUR, BUT YOU ALSO RESENT HIS POPULARITY AND DON'T LIKE THE FACT THAT HE'S GOING OUT WITH A GIRL YOU HAVE A LONG-STANDING CRUSH ON.

WHAT?

NO. NO, THAT'S TOTALLY WRONG. THAT'S **WAY** OFF.

2/6

WELL, I THOUGHT IT MIGHT BE.

WHERE'S ALL THE STUFF I TOLD YOU ABOUT HOW **ANNOYING** ARTUR IS?

MAYBE THE SCHOOL COUNSELLOR WAS RIGHT. SHE SAID I SHOULD STOP CHASING AFTER JENNY.

YES! FINALLY!!

SO YOU'RE ACTUALLY GOING TO ACCEPT THE FACT THAT JENNY AND ARTUR ARE A COUPLE?

YEAH, I THINK I'LL STEP ASIDE. IT'S THE RIGHT THING TO DO.

IT MEANS I'M PUTTING **JENNY'S** HAPPINESS AHEAD OF MY **OWN!** IT'S A VERY UNSELFISH MOVE ON MY PART! VERY NOBLE!

$\frac{2}{9}$

© 2010 by UFS, Inc.

...AND MAYBE JENNY WILL **SEE** HOW NOBLE I AM, AND THEN SHE'LL FALL MADLY IN LOVE WITH ME AND DUMP ARTUR AND YAK YAK YAK YAK YAK YAK YAK YAK YAK

JUST SHOOT ME.

© 2010 by UFS, Inc.

OOH! MR GALVIN'S PASSING BACK OUR RESEARCH PAPERS!

AH! HERE COMES MY A-PLUS!

AN **A-PLUS**? *SNORT!* DREAM **ON**!

LISTEN, GINA, WITH A TOPIC LIKE **MINE**, AN A-PLUS IS A **LOCK**!

OH, YEAH? WHAT WAS YOUR TOPIC?

THE AMAZING **TRUE** STORY OF **JOJO**, THE DOG-FACED BOY!

PLATE 1

WHAT?? THE ASSIGNMENT WAS TO WRITE SOMETHING ABOUT THE **IMMUNE SYSTEM**!!

GINA! **DUH**!

1/31

THE GUY WAS, LIKE, HALF MAN, HALF DOG! HE **OBVIOUSLY** CAUGHT SOME SORT OF CANINE **VIRUS**!

THAT'S IMMUNE SYSTEM STUFF, RIGHT?

OH, GOODY! I GOT AN "A"!

HUH. AN **ALMOST** PERFECT GRADE!

WELL, WHERE'S YOUR **A-PLUS**, GENIUS? MR GALVIN DIDN'T EVEN GIVE YOU BACK YOUR **PAPER**!

...PROBABLY BECAUSE HE'S ABOUT TO GIVE ME SOME SORT OF SPECIAL AWARD!

COME WITH ME, NATE. WE'RE GOING TO SEE THE PRINCIPAL...

HA! HEAR THAT, GINA? **TOLD** YA!

187

188

BE SEATED

I'M NOT SURE I LIKE THIS NEW SEATING ARRANGEMENT.

I **USED** TO SIT BEHIND **CHESTER**. HE'S SO HUGE, I COULD HIDE BEHIND HIM WHENEVER MRS GODFREY WAS CALLING ON PEOPLE!

2/17

BUT I CAN'T HIDE BEHIND **YOU**, CHAD! YOU'RE **TINY!** YOU HAVEN'T GROWN SINCE **FOURTH GRADE!**

MY GRAMMY ALWAYS SAYS "FIRST TO RIPEN, FIRST TO ROT"!

THAT'S NOT HELPING ME, DUDE. SERIOUSLY, CAN YOU SIT ON A PHONE BOOK OR SOMETHING?

READY FOR THE SOCIAL STUDIES TEST?

AM I EVER!

I REVIEWED ALL THE TESTS MRS GODFREY'S GIVEN US THIS YEAR, AND YOU KNOW WHAT I FOUND? A **PATTERN!**

ON EVERY SINGLE TEST, THE SAME SEQUENCE OF ANSWERS SHOWS UP!

I MEMORIZED IT! IT GOES: C,A,A,D,B,C,B, D,C,A,C,B!

SO ALL I HAVE TO DO IS WRITE DOWN **THOSE** LETTERS IN **THAT** ORDER...

SLAM!

...AND I'M BASICALLY **GUARANTEED** AN A-PLUS!

IT'S AN ESSAY TEST.

© 2010 by UFS, Inc.

ANNNNND... BEGIN.

OH, HOW I HATE HER.

196

WHAT'S YOUR POINT?

© 2010 by UFS, Inc.

WHY ARE YOU CARRYING THAT THING AROUND?

THIS "**THING**," FRANCIS, IS MY PRESIDENTIAL **GAVEL!**

IT'S A **SYMBOL** OF THE RESPECT I COMMAND AS CLASS PRESIDENT!

HEY, WHO'S THE DORK WITH THE DOLL HAMMER?

HA HA HA A HA HA

IT'S ALSO GOOD FOR HITTING PEOPLE.

WE WILL ROCK YOU

ALL RIGHT, WE'LL AGREE TO PUT THE BAND BACK TOGETHER... AS LONG AS YOU DON'T GET CARRIED AWAY!

DON'T TURN THIS INTO SOME BIG **EVENT!** DON'T ACT LIKE WE'RE ON OUR WAY TO THE ROCK AND ROLL HALL OF FAME!

LET'S JUST HAVE **FUN**, OK?

OK?

SORRY. JUST WRITING THE LINER NOTES FOR OUR "GREATEST HITS" BOX SET.

YOU KNOW, GUYS, ONCE WE START PLAYING GIGS, WE'RE GONNA NEED STUFF TO SELL TO OUR FANS!

I'M GOING TO DESIGN AN OFFICIAL "ENSLAVE THE MOLLUSK" LOGO FOR POSTERS, T-SHIRTS AND ALL THAT JAZZ!

EXCEPT... HMM... I DON'T KNOW HOW TO DRAW A MOLLUSC.

JUST DRAW ANY RANDOM BIVALVE.

3/6

THANKS, FRANCIS. WHAT GREAT ADVICE.

LET'S CHANGE OUR NAME TO SOMETHING EASIER TO DRAW.

Peirce

I THOUGHT YOU WERE SKATING.

I DIDN'T EVEN MAKE IT TO THE POND. IT'S TOO COLD.

TOO **COLD?** OH, COME **ON!**

WHEN I WAS YOUR AGE, I'D SKATE FOR **HOURS** ON DAYS LIKE THIS!

REALLY?

ABSO-LUTELY!

I'LL JUST TEXT GRAMPS TO CONFIRM.

TIK TIK TIK TIK TIK

✳boop✳

HE SAYS ON COLD DAYS YOU'D PRETEND TO BE SICK SO YOU COULD STAY INSIDE AND PLAY WITH LEGOS.

3/7

© 2010 UFS, Inc.

SON, YOUR GRANDFATHER IS OLD AND SENILE.

DID THEY EVEN **HAVE** LEGOS BACK THEN?

CAPTION ACTION

Ready, set, write! Come up with cool captions for Nate's sketches.

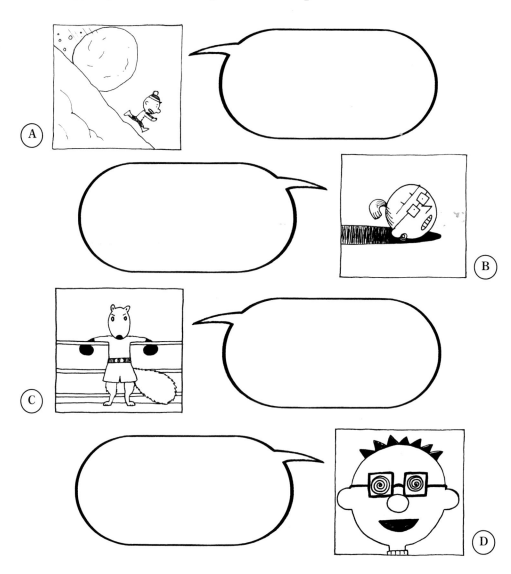

EXTRA CREDIT! Match each sketch to the original comic.

Comic A goes on page _____.

Comic B goes on page _____.

Comic C goes on page _____.

Comic D goes on page _____.

FAST FORWARD

What's going to happen next? It's up to you!

A

Can I help you, sir?

Yes, you can DROP AND GIVE ME TWENTY!

CUSTOMER SERVICE

B

C

Bonus: Can you match each sketch to its Sunday strip?

Comic A goes on page _____.

Comic B goes on page _____.

Comic C goes on page _____.

ALL ABOUT YOU!

Nate loves sports, Spitsy (most of the time), and Jenny.
How about you?

NATE	YOU
	Favourite sport
	Favourite animal
	Favourite friend (or crush!)

BRAIN BOWL

Nate's brain is
filled with trivia!

Now write down all the things running through *your* brain.

LIVIN' LARGE!

P.S. 38 is pretty small. Everyone knows everyone else. So whenever a new kid shows up, it's a major event. Especially when he's got a name like **THIS**:

Anyway, Principal Nichols asked me to be the kid's "buddy," so it's my job to help him make friends...

...and to show him around the school, which is falling apart. That's what happens when a building is one hundred years old.

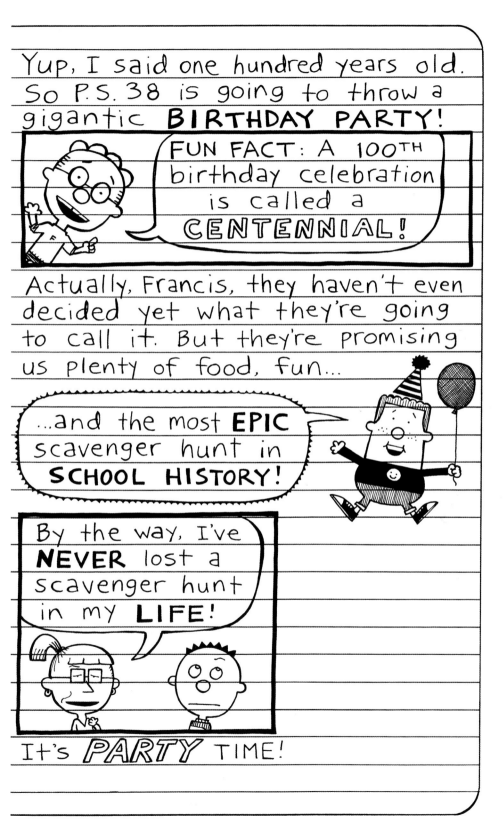

CHECK OUT MORE
BiG NATE

Lincoln Peirce

(pronounced "purse") is a cartoonist/writer and author of the *New York Times* bestselling Big Nate series, now published in twenty-five countries. He is also the creator of the comic strip *Big Nate*, which appears in more than 250 U.S. newspapers and online daily at www.bignate.com.

Lincoln loves comics, ice hockey, and Cheez Doodles (and dislikes cats, figure skating, and egg salad). Just like Nate.

Check out Big Nate Island at www.poptropica.com. And link to www.bignatebooks.com for more information about the author and the Big Nate series, app, audio, and ebooks. Lincoln Peirce lives with his wife and two children in Portland, Maine.